This Winnie-the-Pooh book belongs to

. . . .

. . . .

Be Kind to Bees

In this story Pooh learns all that he can about bees,

so he can make things better for the bees

that live in the Hundred Acre Wood.

This book also contains lots of bee facts and tips

from The British Beekeepers Association,

so you can help bees that live near you too.

Read on to find out more!

Winnie-the-Pooh

Helps the Bees!

Farshore

One hot summer morning, a loud sound

woke Winnie-the-Pooh.

GRRROOWWLL! GURGLE!

He wondered what had made such a noise.

GRRROOWWLL! GURGLE!

it went again, and Pooh realised it was

his very own tummy!

"Time for a little something to eat," he said.

But, as Pooh peered into his last honeypot,

he remembered the tasty smackerel

he'd enjoyed the night before.

"Bother," Pooh frowned at the empty pot.

"I'd better ask the bees for more honey.

Perhaps Piglet can come too."

"Tresspassers will be P-"

"**Something awful has happened!**"
Pooh told Piglet, when he opened his door.

"**Oh no!**" replied a **worried** Piglet.

"I've **run out** of honey!" added Pooh.

Piglet was relieved that nothing **worse** had happened.

"I'll help you get more **honey**," he told Pooh.

But the bees weren't all **buzzing**

around the **Bee Tree** like they usually did.

After carefully climbing up to look in the hole,

Pooh was disappointed to see that the bees

hadn't made much **honey** either!

"I don't think they're **happy**," said Piglet.

"You're right," said Pooh, looking **puzzled.**

"Let's find out how we can cheer them up!"

Roo, Tigger and Kanga were bouncing in the Sandy Place
when Pooh asked what they knew about bees.

"They go **BUZZ! BUZZ!**" shouted Roo.

"They're **stripy** like me!" added Tigger.

"The **Queen bee** is bigger than the other bees," said Kanga.

Pooh thanked them and went off to **find out more.**

Rabbit made a long list of the **bee facts**
he knew, then **slowly** read them
all out to Pooh and Piglet.
"Bees' homes are called **hives**, although the
Hundred Acre Wood bees live in the **Bee Tree,**

where they make **tasty honey,**" he added.

Pooh was beginning to feel **rather sleepy**
by the time Rabbit had **finished** talking.

"Thank you, Rabbit," he yawned, as he went on his way.

Eeyore didn't know much about bees,

but watching the **cool river** flowing past

his **Gloomy Place** he said,

"Maybe the bees are feeling **thirsty**

in this **hot weather**, Pooh?"

"**Eyore,**" Pooh replied, looking very impressed,

"**that is very Good Thinking!**"

Being **awfully clever**, Owl knew all about bees.

"They need **flowers** to make honey and they move **pollen** between plants to help them grow," he said.

"Which flowers do they like?" asked Pooh.

"Many different ones," Owl told him, "including **lavender, sunflowers and cosmos.**"

But the flowers in the wood were **drying up** in the **heat.** That was a **big** problem for the bees!

Lavender

Sunflowers

Cosmos

HOW BEES

2. Bees collect sweet nectar from flowers.

1. Bees fly to flowers.

Christopher Robin had a book about bees. "Bees collect a sweet liquid called **nectar** from flowers and store it in **honeycombs** to make honey!" he told Pooh.

MAKE HONEY

3. Bees take nectar to their hive or tree.

4. They store nectar in the honeycomb to make delicious honey.

Pooh knew that bees needed lots of **flowers** to be **happy** and he'd be happy **too**, when they made **lots of honey** again!

Pooh thought about what he'd **learnt about bees** ...

In hot weather they need to drink more **water**.

They need **flowers** to collect nectar and pollen.

They live in **hives** or **trees**, where they make honey.

His friends all agreed to **help the bees.**

First, they dipped **watering cans**

in the river, so they could water the

thirsty flowers in the wood.

Then, Pooh and Rabbit **planted more flowers** by the Bee Tree and Piglet and Kanga put **flowerpots** on their windowsills.

Eeyore and Tigger filled some bowls with **water** and **stones**,

so the bees could **drink more** water

in the hot weather without swimming too!

And Owl and Roo made **colourful posters** to **cheer up the bees!**

Soon the bees were **happier than ever** and making lots of **tasty honey!**

"Three cheers for bees!" said Christopher Robin.

"**Hooray** for **Pooh** and **bees!**" they all cheered together.

Poster fun!

Pooh and his friends made bee posters. Ask an adult to help stick the double-sided poster opposite in your window to spread the important message to help bees.

You can make your own posters too. Don't forget to write inspiring words like

SAVE OUR BEES,
BEE KIND or
BE A HONEY HERO!

BEE
KIND

© Disney

Farshore

First published in Great Britain 2021 by Farshore
An imprint of HarperCollins*Publishers*
1 London Bridge Street, London SE1 9GF
www.farshore.co.uk

HarperCollins*Publishers*
1st Floor, Watermarque Building, Ringsend Road
Dublin 4, Ireland

Written by Catherine Shoolbred
Designed by Pritty Ramjee
Illustrations by Eleanor Taylor and Mikki Butterley

With special thanks to Anne Rowberry of The British Beekeepers Association
for her valuable insight and assistance with the creation of this book.

ISBN 978 0 7555 0067 3
Printed in Italy
001

Parental guidance is advised for all craft and colouring activities. Always ask an adult to help
when using glue, paint and scissors. Wear protective clothing and cover surfaces to avoid staining.

Stay safe online. Farshore is not responsible for content hosted by third parties.

Farshore takes its responsibility to the planet and its inhabitants very seriously.
We aim to use papers from well-managed forests run by responsible suppliers.
This bee-friendly book has been printed using vegetable-based inks on FSC-approved papers.

FSC
www.fsc.org

MIX
Paper from
responsible sources
FSC™ C007454

This book is produced from independently certified FSC™ paper
to ensure responsible forest management.

For more information visit: www.harpercollins.co.uk/green

Did You Know ...?

Bees sleep — Walter Kaiser, a bee researcher, spotted that bees can sleep for up to 8 hours a day!

Solitary bees — who live on their own in holes in the ground, in walls or in man-made bee hotels.

Bees make other things beyond honey including ...
Propolis — bees use it to fill holes in their hive. It helps people with sore throats and toothache.

Bee bread — is a mix of plant pollen and honey. It helps Olympic athletes perform even better!

There are many types of bees including ...
Bumblebees — who make a loud buzzing noise as they fly and spread pollen between flowers.

Royal Jelly — is fed to baby queen bees. It helps people with everything from hay fever to broken bones!

Honey bees — who collect sweet nectar from flowers and store it in honeycombs to make honey.